Weekly Reader Children's Book Club presents

The MOON SINGER

The Moon Singer

By Clyde Robert Bulla

Illustrated by Trina Schart Hyman

Thomas Y. Crowell Company
New York

To Jean Maloney

LONG AGO, in a far country, there lived a miller and his wife. One day a woman came to the mill, leading a child by the hand.

"Take this boy," she said. "I can no longer care for him."

"Another mouth to feed? Oh, no," said the miller.

"Then," said the woman, "at least give us a place to rest tonight."

The miller gave them a bed of straw in the mill shed. In the morning the woman was gone. The child was left behind.

"This is not so bad," said the miller's wife. "He may be a help to us later on."

"That's true," said the miller. So they kept the boy and called him Torr, which was a short name and easy to remember.

He grew tall and strong, and he worked about the mill.

But he was a strange boy.

Sometimes he forgot his work and wandered off into the woods. There he would stand, listening, as if he heard something no one else could hear.

Sometimes at night he left his bed and stood for hours under the sky.

On a summer night the miller and his wife wakened to the sound of singing. The voice was clear and high. The song was one they had never heard before.

They went to the window.

"It's Torr!" said the miller's wife.

The boy was standing in the moonlight. He was singing, with his face turned toward the sky.

The miller ran out in his nightshirt. "Stop your noise!" he said. "You'll wake the whole village!"

He dragged Torr inside. He shook him and boxed his ears.

After that the boy sang no more where the miller and his wife might hear. Late at night he went deep into the woods, and there he sang.

A hunter heard him and drew near to listen.

Afterward he talked in the village of the boy who sang. "His music sends chills down my spine," he said, "but I would go a long way to hear it."

Others went to the woods to listen.

"The boy is mad," said some of them. "He may bring harm to us."

"He has a great gift," said the old music-master who lived in the village. "He cannot sing at home, so he sings in the woods, and where is the harm in that?"

One evening a stranger came to the village. A wheel of his carriage had broken. While it was being mended, he stopped at the inn.

Villagers gathered to see him. He was so richly dressed that they were sure he must be a fine gentleman.

One of them asked, "Sir, are you a lord?"

The man laughed. "As a matter of fact, I
am," he said. "I am Lord Crail, from the court
of the queen."

"Ah!" said the people, all together. A woman
asked, "Is the queen as beautiful as they say?"

"Even more beautiful," said Lord Crail.

"And is the palace really so splendid?" asked
the woman.

"The most splendid of all palaces," said
Lord Crail.

"I once heard," said the woman, "of a baker who made such pies that he was taken to the palace to bake for the queen."

"This is true enough," said Lord Crail. "And the best storytellers in the land, the best music makers, actors, and dancers are all at the palace. If they do not come to us, we find them and bring them there."

The old music-master had come to the inn with the others. He asked, "My lord, does the queen have need of a singer?"

"There are singers at court," said Lord Crail, "but the queen has grown weary of them. She says their songs all sound the same." He asked, "Is there a singer in your village?"

"There is, my lord," said the music-master. "He is a boy who sings in the woods at night."

"That boy is mad!" said some of the others.

"I find no madness in him," said the music-master. "His voice touches the heart, and the songs he sings are like no other songs."

"When may I hear him?" asked Lord Crail.

"He sings in the woods when the moon is shining," said the music-master. "The moon will be shining tonight."

"Take me to hear him," said Lord Crail.

They went together to the woods.

"Just ahead is a bridge over the stream," said the music-master. "The boy often goes there to sing."

"Listen!" said Lord Crail.

Deep in the woods the boy was singing. There were no words to the song. The tune rose and fell and rose again, like the song of a bird.

Lord Crail started forward. Dry sticks cracked under his feet. When he reached the bridge, the boy was gone.

"He heard us and ran away," said the music-master. "He is very shy."

"I must find him," said Lord Crail.

"Nothing easier," said the music-master. "He works at the mill."

The next day Lord Crail went to the mill. There he found Torr carrying sacks of flour into the shed.

"I heard you sing last night," said Lord Crail.

Torr looked away.

"Come, don't be afraid," said Lord Crail. "Who taught you to sing?"

"No one," answered Torr.

"Where do you learn your songs?" asked Lord Crail.

"They come to me," said the boy. "When I'm alone they come to me."

"Why do you hide away in the woods?" asked Lord Crail. "Why not sing where everyone can hear you?"

Torr looked surprised. "Who would want to hear me?" he asked.

"Perhaps the queen herself," said Lord Crail. "Today I shall take you away from here. We shall go to Her Majesty."

"Where?" asked Torr.

"To the palace," said Lord Crail. "To the queen."

The miller had been listening. He spoke up. "My lord, how can we ever thank you? My wife and I have brought up the boy as if he were our own. We always knew there were great things in store for him. Tell me, will he live in the palace?"

"Most likely," said Lord Crail.

"Will he be paid well?" asked the miller.

"He will live just like a prince," said Lord Crail.

"Do you hear?" said the miller to the boy. "And when you are living like a prince, think of my wife and me, who were always so kind to you."

The carriage came for Torr and Lord Crail. Torr had had no time to think. He could not believe what was happening. On the long journey his head was in a whirl.

They came to the palace with its stone walls and great iron gates.

Lord Crail led the way down a long hall and into a room. "You will sleep here," he said.

But Torr could not sleep. The bed was too large and too soft. The air was heavy. It was hard for him to breathe.

In the morning servants came into the room. They combed his hair and curled it with hot irons. They fitted him into a tight suit of crimson velvet. They pushed his feet into shoes that pinched his toes.

Lord Crail came in.

"Now," he said, "you are ready to meet the queen."

Torr followed him up the stairs and into the music room. Lords and ladies were there. The queen sat among them, in a chair higher than those of the others. She was young and lovely. Her dark hair was caught up in a gold band that looked like a crown.

Torr knelt before her, as he had been told to do.

"Lord Crail says he found you singing to the moon," she said. "Will you sing to me now?"

Torr stood before the queen. He felt cold, and he trembled. He opened his mouth, and no sound came.

"Sing!" said Lord Crail in a fierce whisper.

Again Torr tried. His throat was dry, and no song came to him.

Lord Crail bowed to the queen. "Your Majesty, the boy is not quite ready," he said. "After he has rested, I promise you he will sing even better than ever. Let me bring him before you tomorrow."

He took Torr away.

The next day they went back to the music room. The queen was there alone.

"I thought it might be easier," she said, "if the boy sang only for me."

"Your Majesty is most kind," said Lord Crail. He said to Torr, "Sing."

"I can't!" said Torr.

"You must!" said Lord Crail.

Torr's mouth opened. One strange sound came out, like the croaking of a frog.

Lord Crail caught Torr's arm and led him away. He said to the boy, when they were alone, "I brought you here. I promised the queen you would sing such songs as she had never heard before. Why have you made a fool of me?"

Torr said nothing.

"Answer me!" said Lord Crail.

"I—don't know," said Torr.

"You don't know—you don't know!" said Lord Crail. "Is that all you can say? The queen was waiting. I was waiting. You have made a fool of me!" He went away.

Soon a servant came into the room. He stripped off Torr's velvet suit and gave him back the clothes he had worn to the palace.

"What am I to do?" asked Torr.

"You're to go," said the servant.

Torr left the palace. He went out into the city. All about him were horses and carriages and crowds of people.

He walked up one street and down another. He tried to find his way out of the city. At last he was in the country, on the road that led to his village.

At night he slept by the road. Toward the end of the next day he was back in his village.

He went to the mill. The miller and his wife were there. They were painting a sign to hang over the door.

Once the mill had had no name. Now they had given it one. They were painting the sign to read: "The Mill of the Queen's Singer."

They stared at Torr.

"You're home!" said the miller's wife.

"Why aren't you in the palace?" asked the miller.

"They sent me away," said Torr.

"Didn't you go there to be the queen's singer?" asked the miller.

"Yes," said Torr, "but—I couldn't sing."

"Why not?" asked the miller's wife.

"I don't know," said Torr. "The walls shut me in, and the air pressed down on me, and I couldn't sing."

"You didn't try," said the miller. "You had no trouble singing before. Then when you had this great chance, you didn't try."

"You must go back," said the miller's wife.

"No," said Torr. "I can't ever go back."

"What shall we do?" cried the miller's wife. "We've told everyone our boy is singer to the queen. We even named the mill for him. After all our years of hard work, we thought life was going to be easier." She said to Torr, "All you've done for us is make us look like fools. Now you can go!"

"Yes, go!" said the miller.

"Where?" asked Torr.

"I don't care," said the miller. "Just go!"

Angrily he picked up a pot of paint and
threw it at the boy. The lid came off the pot.
The paint splashed Torr from head to foot.

He turned and ran.

He ran out of the village. He was a strange,
wild-looking figure with green paint on his
face and clothes.

"See the green-faced scarecrow!" people said,
and they drove him away.

He hid in barns and haystacks. He ate what little food he could find—a few berries here, a sour apple there.

He came to the hill country where shepherds cared for their flocks. He was ill and half starved. He lay down to rest.

A storm came. Still he lay there, too ill to move.

A shepherd and his wife found him and carried him to their hut. The shepherd's wife fed him. The shepherd scrubbed the last of the paint from his face.

Torr stayed in the hut until he grew strong again. He helped the shepherds care for their sheep.

Sometimes he remembered the mill and the miller and his wife. He remembered Lord Crail and the palace and the queen.

Always he tried to put these thoughts out of his mind. They were like bad dreams to him now.

The shepherds were kind to him. He liked to be among the sheep and lambs, and he made friends with the shepherds' dogs.

He said to himself, "I am happy here."

Yet it was not true. He was not quite happy. Over and over he asked himself the reason.

One night he could not sleep. He went out into the woods. The moon was bright. A breeze blew, and he could smell the leaves and grass and the sea beyond.

Suddenly he was happy. He thought he had never been so happy before. A song had come to him.

He began to sing. His voice was clear. It

was stronger and deeper than before. He
wanted to go leaping from hill to hill.
He wanted to shout, "I can sing—
I can sing again!"

For half the night he sang. The shepherds
came to their doors and listened in wonder.

Night after night Torr sang.

Word traveled across the land of the
singing shepherd boy. A traveler brought the
word to Lord Crail at the queen's palace.

"He sings at night?" asked Lord Crail.

"Yes," said the traveler. "They call him the
moon singer, because they say he sings
to the moon."

"Does he have another name?" asked
Lord Crail.

"Yes," said the traveler. "It is Torr."

Lord Crail went to the queen. "Do you
remember the boy who came here to sing,
Your Majesty?" he asked. "The one who
opened his mouth and croaked like a frog?"

"I remember him well," said the queen.

"He was only pretending," said Lord Crail.
"All the time he could sing. He is singing
now in another part of the country."

"Why should he pretend he could not sing?" asked the queen.

"I mean to find out," said Lord Crail. "I mean to bring him here again. If he dares to pretend, he will be punished in a way he won't forget."

"The boy did not seem to be pretending," said the queen.

"Your Majesty, he must have been," said Lord Crail.

"I can't believe it," said the queen, "and as much as I wish to hear him, it doesn't seem right to bring him here again."

"Then how can you hope to hear him?" asked Lord Crail.

"I could go to him, instead," she said.

"Your Majesty!" cried Lord Crail. "You could not do that!"

"Surely the queen may do as she wishes," she said. "I have stayed so long inside these walls that I am weary of them. Find out where the boy lives, and we shall go there."

So it was that the queen set out on a journey with two ladies of the court, Lord Crail, and three servants.

They traveled until they came to the hill country. Then they hid the royal coach in an old barn. They dressed in the plain clothes of country people.

They found the house where Torr lived. The queen said to the shepherd, "We have heard of the boy who sings. When may we hear him?"

"In a little while, when the moon rises," said the shepherd. "Take the path to the clearing in the woods. Many go there to listen, but they keep themselves hidden, because the boy is shy."

The queen and her party went down the path and into the woods. When they came to the clearing, they waited in the shadows. Others were waiting, too. Shepherds were there with their wives and children.

The moon rose. By its light they saw the boy in the clearing. He began to sing.

"Oh—beautiful!" whispered the queen.

"You see," Lord Crail whispered back. "All the time he could sing. He shall be brought to the palace and—"

"No," said the queen. "Can't you see? He belongs here."

"But Your Majesty, you have a right to hear him whenever you wish," said Lord Crail.

"So I do," said the queen, "and so I shall. Hush! He's beginning again."

Torr's song floated up through the woods. It was a song of the night—of the moon and the stars and mist over the sea.

"Beautiful!" the queen whispered again.

So she listened, that night and many another night. And Torr sang his songs, never knowing she was near.

ABOUT THE AUTHOR

Clyde Robert Bulla was born near King City, Missouri. He received his early education in a one-room schoolhouse, where he began writing stories and songs. After several years as a writer of magazine stories, he finished his first book, then went to work on a newspaper.

He continued to write, and his books for children became so successful that he was able to satisfy his desire to travel through the United States, Mexico, Hawaii, and Europe. He now lives in Los Angeles.

In 1962, Mr. Bulla received the first award of the Southern California Council on Children's Literature for distinguished contributions to that field. He has written more than thirty stories for young readers.

ABOUT THE ILLUSTRATOR

Trina Schart Hyman and her young daughter live in Lime, New Hampshire, in a one-hundred-and-fifty-year-old house on the banks of the Connecticut River. Mrs. Hyman enjoys gardening, walking, and canoeing. She is also a devoted cyclist, having once undertaken a 2,800-mile wheeling trip through Sweden, Norway, and Denmark.

Mrs. Hyman was born in Philadelphia and attended the Philadelphia Museum College of Art and the Museum School of Fine Arts in Boston. She then lived for a while in Stockholm, Sweden, where she studied advertising at the Swedish State Art School for Applied Arts.

One of Mrs. Hyman's lithographs received first prize in the Boston Arts Festival. She is the illustrator of many books for young people.